WARNING

This book contains sexually explicit scenes and adult language. It may be considered offensive to some readers. This book is for sale to adults ONLY.

* * * * * * * * * * * * * * * * * *

Please store your files wisely where they cannot be accessed by underage readers.

ISBN-13: 978-1987863215
ISBN-10: 1987863216

Other Books by Darla Dunbar:

<u>The Romeo Alpha BBW Paranormal Shifter Romance Series</u>

Amanda Walker thinks that she has a normal and boring life. That is until after her 24th birthday. Everything changes when she meets the man who says he was supposed to be her husband. Denying everything the man says, she fights him every step of the way. But after he kidnaps her, Amanda discovers that there are some things about her family that her parents kept a secret all these years. Among the history of the family she learns secrets she thought only happened in story books. Can Amanda tell the difference between truth and lies or is she this mysterious woman that holds the key to a legacy?

<u>Romeo Alpha Blood Lines Romance Series</u>

Twenty-four years have passed in relative peace for Amanda and Romeo. They've raised five children into adulthood and are thoroughly enjoying their lives as the Alpha King and Queen of the werewolves. At twenty-four, Sarina is just stepping into her powers and will be ripe for mating when her birthday comes in two weeks. What no one knows is the danger that lurks just outside their tight knit community. Romeo has made peace with the other clans and has enjoyed that peace, but it will all come crashing down around him when his oldest daughter comes of age to take a mate.

<u>The Alpha Feud BBW Paranormal Shifter Romance
Series</u>

Eliza's life consisted of reporting on boring, crowd-pleasing events, like their country livestock fair. With the arrival of two handsome brothers, the lives of Eliza and her best friend, Melissa, are shaken to the core. For Eliza, the arrival of this new man becomes a test of her relationship with her current boyfriend, who she's been happily living with for over six years. Does Hayden, a complete stranger, really wield the power to make Eliza reconsider her relationship with Andrew?

<u>The Alpha Packed BBW Paranormal Shifter
Romance Series</u>

Darlene has led a quiet life since suffering through a terrible break-up. She wants nothing more than to spend her time in front of the TV, away from any sort of trouble. But all that goes down the drain when handsome, rugged and rough Idris comes into her life. He is a werewolf on the lookout for his missing pack leader. Darlene quickly finds herself pulled towards this mysterious man and at the same time finds herself falling deeper and deeper into the world of the supernatural.

<u>The Daemon Paranormal Romance Chronicles</u>

The daemon infighting can only be stopped when a strong leader emerges to calm the different factions. Juno appears to be at the heart of the conflict. Things become complicated when Phoebe and Supay try to negotiate with the siren, Juno. The love triangle among Phoebe, Supay and Apollo become tense when Juno's meddling threatens to destroy any romance that develops.

<u>The Mind Talker Paranormal Romance Series</u>

Ananda finds herself on the run and she's not alone. With help from Jared, a stranger that she just met, the two evade capture by an organization that is intent on hunting her kind. Ananda and Jared are able to read minds. When an unfortunate incident happened involving a disturbed individual that resulted in the death of his schoolmates, the secret organization decided to take action.

Get the latest update on new releases from the author at:

https://darladunbar.com/newsletter/

This book is Part Four of "<u>The Leather Satchel Paranormal Romance Series</u>"

Book 1 - Valtina's Redemption

Valtina is stuck in Middle World, unable to pass on to The Afterlife. In order to redeem herself from past deeds done, she must help bring romance back into the world and stop The Dark Side from destroying love in its entirety. Following orders issued by Ladaya and armed with a leather satchel filled with the appropriate tools and weapons, Valtina must bring romance back into the lives of Samantha and Joshua, thereby saving their marriage.

Book 2 - Unfaithful

Amy and Matt's relationship was never meant to be. The evil forces at work are bent on eliminating love on Earth. Couples are being mismatched in order to create chaos. It is Valtina's mission the help Amy find her soul mate and repair the damage that is being caused by the dark forces.

Book 3 - Evil Lust

Henry and Claire are meant to be together. But a succubus has taken over Henry's actions. Under her spell, Henry has succumbed to lusting after Charlotte, the human form that the succubus has assumed. If Claire were to find out, then their marriage will be ruined beyond repair. It is up to Valtina to break the succubus' spell and clear Henry's memory of any guilt that would haunt his love for Claire forever.

Book 4 - Salvaged Soul Mates

The Dark Side is winning. A Mystic has organized the evil monsters to steal every soul on Earth and leave it loveless. It is up to Valtina to do her part to save the human race. Sent by Ladaya back to Earth, Valtina's job is to unite a mismatched couple with their true soul-mates. Sebastian and Claudia were not meant to be married to each other. But a trickster was involved in encouraging the mismatch. Searching through her leather satchel, Valtina found the tools needed to do the job.

Book 5 - Fury of Lust

Valtina's missions are becoming more dangerous and will need the protection of a warrior and emere while out on duty. This time she needs to rid Rachel of a fury and free Sean of his demons. Rachel and Sean are meant to be true lovers but they have been prevented from meeting each other. Valtina must use the arsenal in her leather satchel to ensure that true love follows its course when Rachel and Sean finally meet.

Book 6 - True Lovers

Middle World has been invaded by the wraiths. While the Generals battle the monsters to protect Middle World, Valtina must continue her missions to save love on Earth. The evil forces have brain-washed Penelope and Davis into thinking that their attraction for each other is wrong. Valtina's mission is to clear the way for the couple to see that they were meant for each other and to let true love runs its fateful course.

The Leather Satchel Paranormal Romance Series

Salvaged Soul Mates

Book Four

By Darla Dunbar

Copyright Revelry Publishing 2015

Table of Contents

Chapter One

VALTINA SAT under a tree in Middle World, observing the spirits around her. She'd been scanning the faces of those who passed ever since Ladaya had told her that her soul-mate was also stuck in Middle World. She tried to sense his spirit, but as her mentor had warned, she hadn't recognized him yet. Valtina contented herself to sitting still and watching as the others moved about. Like her, many had been enlisted to fight in the war against evil. Middle World was frequently filled with visitors from The Afterlife. Generals, like Ladaya, popped in to give instructions and updates to their soldiers. Valtina hadn't seen anyone she recognized, though several of her friends had already moved on.

As Valtina waited she thought about her mission. The last one had been more difficult than the previous one, as she'd had to break the spell of a succubus. And Ladaya had warned her that all varieties of monsters were fighting for the other side. She wondered what kind of danger she would encounter next. Valtina's thoughts were interrupted when Ladaya appeared before her. She was frazzled, and seemed to be on the verge of tears.

"Ladaya! What's happened?" Valtina asked in a panic.

"I've just been observing," Ladaya sobbed, "the mist… the black mist of evil… it's growing. I watched it spread before my eyes. Oh Valtina, I don't know what we're going to do."

"Do you know what's making it spread so quickly?"

"We do. One of our under-covers reported in yesterday, and confirmed our worst fear. The driving force behind the other army is a creature that was believed to be a thing of legend. No one in my time, or the times of those before me, has ever encountered one. It is a thing so evil it cannot be killed. Part demon, part witch, she's rumored to be the spawn of a warlock and something very unnatural he conjured in his bedroom. Her powers are innumerable, and, I'm afraid, impossible to defeat. She's bred a wraith army; their sole purpose is to steal every soul on Earth. As you know, without a soul, one cannot feel love. If we don't stop them soon, it will all be over." Ladaya sighed.

"This creature… you don't mean a Mystic?!" Valtina asked with alarm.

"I'm afraid so." Ladaya nodded. "They call her Morgonda. We're quite certain she's the one who organized the monsters against us. Her goal is to rid the world of living creatures, and reign as Queen of the monsters.

"What can I do?" Valtina asked quickly. "How can we defeat them? Tell me how, Ladaya. Surely we need everyone focused on this right now. I can fix people's love lives once we've defeated them!"

"Valtina, I appreciate your offer. But it's important that we take advantage of each spirit's strengths. We have others who are more fitted to destroying evil, and you are too valuable in your area for us to risk you! But be aware, the wraiths can see you. Remember, their sole purpose is to steal souls… As you are nothing but a soul, you'd be an easy job for them. But, as usual, should you encounter one, help will appear."

"That's ridiculous, Ladaya," Valtina argued. "Don't the 'qualified' spirits have more important things to do than rescue me? Tell me how to take them out myself," she insisted.

Ladaya sighed. "Really, Valtina, I don't want you anywhere near them. There are rules for a reason, and you are no exception. And I believe that's one of the things you're in Middle World to work on? Following *directions*?" Ladaya reminded her sharply. Valtina sighed. It was true that in all of her lifetimes, she'd had a bit of a problem following the rules. Even really important rules she'd ignore, just for the sake of ignoring them. The Supreme Ruler in The Afterlife felt she needed some more practice in listening to authority before she moved on.

"I'm sorry, Ladaya. You're right," Valtina conceded. "What are my instructions? What's my next mission? The faster I get started, the faster I can move on to the next one, right?" She smiled.

Ladaya softened. "Well, as I told you, humans are spreading the evil almost as quickly as the monsters. Morgonda has sent these humans helpers, in the form of tricksters. They make sure the humans' plans fall into place, and that the plans of those around them fall apart. I'm afraid they've been at work since long before we knew of The Dark Side's plans. The couple I'm sending you to next has been affected by a trickster for five years. They're a mismatched couple, you see, put together by their fathers as a part of a master business plan. The fathers sold their souls to a demon years ago, in exchange for success in their law firm. One man pressured his son to follow in his footsteps… the other did the same to his daughter. It seemed only natural to the two men that their children should marry, and keep the fortune within the two families. Claudia, the wife, fell in love with a man she met as an undergrad. Albert was smart and handsome, but seeking a teaching degree, which Claudia's father thought beneath his daughter. Sebastian, the husband, hasn't met his soul-mate yet. They were supposed to get together three years ago. So far, she hasn't encountered evil yet, and is still waiting for him.

"The trickster attached to Claudia and Sebastian's fathers put many obstacles in Albert's way, making it seem as if his relationship with Claudia was a lost cause. The trickster also made sure that Sebastian was in the right place at the right time to comfort Claudia after Albert disappeared. Then, the trickster inspired lust between the two. As soon as their fathers realized they were sleeping together, they insisted upon a wedding. The trickster was still doing his job, and inspiring lust between the couple. He's been dealt with, and now we need you to break up Sebastian and Claudia, and reunite them with their soul-mates," Ladaya finished.

"Consider it done, Ladaya," Valtina promised. "I'll return soon. I pray I come back to good news."

"That makes two of us." Ladaya smiled sadly.

Chapter Two

The white fog enveloped Valtina and transported her to Claudia and Sebastian's townhouse. Valtina arrived early on a Saturday afternoon, and found the couple in separate rooms of the house. Claudia sat in the living room, absentmindedly watching a week's worth of recorded television. Valtina entered her mind for a moment. "What in the world has come over me?" Claudia thought. "He's my husband. I *married* him for Christ sake. Why am I suddenly looking at him like he's my brother? What am I going to do?"

Valtina felt sorry for Claudia. She didn't realize that she'd been under the influence of a trickster. All she knew was that suddenly, she wasn't attracted to her husband anymore. Valtina could read that Claudia still loved Sebastian very much, but not in a sexual way. The woman was fighting anxiety over what she would do the next time Sebastian propositioned her. "I just can't do it," she kept thinking to herself over and over again. "But why can't I just do it?" Valtina wanted to take the anxiety from Claudia, but felt it may be best to let it work to her advantage. She left the woman in the living room and glided through the townhouse to find Sebastian.

Valtina found him sitting in his study, attempting to focus on depositions for his upcoming trial. Like his wife, he was distracted by thoughts and feelings he didn't understand. Valtina entered his mind. "It's just a phase," he was assuring himself. "All married couples go through stuff like this. It will pass. We've always had such a hot sex life. We were bound to hit a dry spell at some point." But Valtina could tell that he didn't believe his own reassurances. He was now no more attracted to Claudia than she was to him.

Valtina thought this may be her easiest job yet. With the trickster gone, the couple was sure to part on their own. She wondered why Ladaya hadn't waited until the couple had already split. It seemed all there was for her to do was to sit back and wait until the couple parted. Then she could match them with their soul-mates. Valtina returned to the living room, sat on the couch, and watched television with Claudia for the rest of the day.

Much to Valtina's surprise, the couple carried on as usual on Saturday night and Sunday. They slept curled together in bed, they got up early and attended morning mass, and they dined at the same restaurant they always visited for Sunday brunch. It wasn't until later Sunday afternoon, when Claudia received a phone call from her father that things started to change. Valtina entered her mind, hoping to hear both sides of the conversation. But instead of being able to hear Claudia's father's words, all Valtina heard was the fear and terror in Claudia's mind. "I have to get over this… I have to find a way to make it work with Sebastian… Daddy will never understand… I don't think I could take the lectures from him if I ended things. What would happen to the firm?" Valtina left Claudia's mind… she'd heard all she needed to know. She entered Sebastian's mind and heard similar thoughts about both of their fathers. Valtina realized then why she'd been sent so soon… neither member of the couple would risk their fathers' wrath without some serious inspiration.

Valtina consulted her trusty leather satchel, looking for tools to aid her in her mission. The contents of the satchel changed with every mission. This time she found a college yearbook, a flyer for an art show, and a coupon for free admittance to a local club. Valtina's powers told her that the yearbook and the coupon should be left for Claudia, while the flyer would inspire Sebastian. She spilled a large box in Claudia's closet and placed the yearbook on top of the pile. Then, Valtina placed the flyer in Sebastian's briefcase… the coupon she would hold on to for now.

As Valtina had hoped, Claudia found the yearbook when she went to put away her shoes and lay out clothes for the next day. Valtina felt a sadness wash over Claudia, who quickly hid the book beneath her robe. She poked her head into Sebastian's study on her way to the couple's library.

"I'm not tired. I think I'm going to read for a bit," she told her husband.

"Alright sweetheart," Sebastian replied without looking up. "I'll see you in the morning."

Claudia padded down to the library and curled up on the sofa. She began flipping through the yearbook, pausing longer on some pages than others. Valtina watched tears fill the woman's eyes as she thought about the love she'd lost. Valtina entered Claudia's mind, and found that she'd never understood why Albert disappeared… she'd loved him so deeply. Valtina cleared Claudia's mind and dried her tears.

"There's still a chance," Claudia thought. "I don't know how I know that, but I do. I love him… I still love him so much. But how could it be possible?" Valtina sensed Claudia's thoughts turning to her father. She'd thought long and hard about how to deal with the fathers… how was she supposed to save people who were completely overcome by evil? When the answer finally came to her, she was amazed at how simple it was. She didn't have to do anything to the older men at all. Her job was to save Claudia, Albert, Sebastian, and Lindsey. The fathers weren't her problem. Valtina reentered Claudia's mind and removed the part of her that cared what her father thought.

"Why the hell do I care what he thinks?" Claudia asked herself. "Like he knows anything about love! I've lost count of how many times he's been married. And if it means I have to leave the firm, so be it. I'd rather be happy with Albert and poor than go through the emotions here with all of the money in the world… I miss him so much. How could I not have realized how much?! I'm going to have to break this to Sebastian." Satisfied that Claudia was moving in the right direction, Valtina set off to find Sebastian. He was already sound asleep in the bedroom. Valtina placed a face in his mind… a beautiful woman with fair skin, blonde hair, and clear blue eyes. Sebastian dreamed of her for the rest of the night.

Chapter Three

The next morning, Sebastian woke up and found himself alone in bed. A note on the kitchen counter told him that Claudia had left early for the office. It wasn't unusual for the couple to drive to work separately. Sebastian poured himself a cup of coffee and opened his briefcase to study the notes for the opening statement he was scheduled to make in a few days. Between the first and second page of notes, Sebastian found the flyer for the art gallery showing. He assumed that Claudia had planted it there. Their anniversary was next month, and Claudia always left hints about gifts she wanted. Sebastian decided to visit the gallery over lunch. He felt guilty about a very vivid sexual dream he'd had the night before, that hadn't involved his wife. "Yes, I'll buy her a present… that'll make me feel better," Valtina heard him think to himself. She smiled. If only he knew just how much better he was about to feel.

Claudia had a hard time concentrating at work. Thoughts of Albert and anger toward her father filled her mind, and she realized that she'd been reading the same paragraph of a brief for almost half an hour. "I'm not going to do any good here," she thought to herself. She gave her secretary instructions to cancel her afternoon appointments and to not put any calls through to her cell phone. "Especially my father… and Sebastian," she added. Her secretary nodded with understanding. None of the firm's employees had ever understood how Sebastian or Claudia put up with their fathers. The young couple was so sweet and kind, the complete opposite of the men who raised them. Claudia's secretary promised to tell everyone that she wasn't feeling well, and was not to be disturbed. Relieved, Claudia drove home to contemplate her next step.

Sebastian checked in at his wife's office before lunch and found that she'd left for the day. "I wouldn't bother her until you get home. I think she was planning on taking a nap," her secretary advised. "Perfect," Sebastian thought. "The gallery purchase can double as a get well gift." He smiled to himself as he set off to the gallery.

Valtina stopped at the townhouse to check on Claudia. She was happy to discover the woman spread out on her bed with a large pile of keepsakes from her relationship with Albert. Reminiscing over the objects was building Claudia's resolve for what she had to do next. Valtina sensed that Claudia was worried about Sebastian. They'd grown up together, after all, and had always been close friends. Claudia wasn't looking forward to causing him any pain. If things went as Valtina planned, however, Sebastian would be just as happy about the breakup as Claudia was.

Valtina left the townhouse and arrived at the gallery just as Sebastian drove up. She entered first, and watched Sebastian's mouth drop as he walked in the door. There, behind the counter, stood the blonde woman from his dream.

"Hello," Lindsey greeted him with a smile. "Is there anything I can help you with?"

Several awkward moments passed before Sebastian spoke. "I was thinking of redecorating my office," he said when he finally found his voice. "What pieces would you recommend?" Valtina had been prepared to stop him from mentioning his wife, but she didn't have to. Obviously, true love was working its magic on Sebastian. Valtina observed the two for just a moment before she became distracted by a shadow that fell over the gallery. Just as the diners in the coffee shop hadn't heard the succubus's wail, the gallery shoppers didn't seem to notice the light being drained from the building. Valtina braced herself as a large, black, hooded figure came through the gallery wall. Valtina knew she was looking at a wraith.

Before Valtina had time to gasp, she heard a loud pop and Demetri appeared in the room. He drew a large silver dagger from his robes and swiftly drove it into the wraith's chest. The monster dissolved into thin air, releasing countless rays of silver light.

"Those are the souls it's stolen," Demetri explained, appearing at Valtina's side. "They'll return to their bodies now, and right the wrongs that have been done in their absence. Some of them may need a little extra help though," he added, smiling at Valtina. "I hear you're quite the matchmaker."

Valtina blushed at the compliment. "I just remind people of who they really are, and what they really want," she explained modestly. "What you do is far more important."

"Everyone is important," Demetri said firmly. "We all have unique gifts. And we need all of them if we're going to defeat the evil forces."

"How are things going on your end?" Valtina inquired. "When I last talked to Ladaya, she seemed discouraged."

"With good reason," Demetri sighed. "We're falling fast. Three of my brothers have fallen to wraiths this week. I can only imagine that it's the same for everyone. We're fighting as hard as we can, but the other side is still gaining. It doesn't help that they can breed monsters faster than we can kill them. Our only real hope is to somehow defeat Morgonda. Ladaya and the other generals think their ranks will fall apart without anyone to direct them."

"But how do you kill something that's immortal?" Valtina asked. She shot a quick look to Sebastian and Lindsey, and found them talking intently and gazing into each other's eyes.

"That's what we're trying to figure out," Demetri began. "There's a theory…" He paused for a moment, as a blue mist surrounded him. "I'm needed elsewhere, Valtina," he explained. "I'll see you next time." With a smile, Demetri disappeared. Valtina turned back to Sebastian. Lindsey was writing her phone number on a gallery catalog. With a smile, Sebastian accepted the catalog and promised to return when he'd decided on his paintings. Valtina entered Sebastian's mind as he drove back to the townhouse.

"How is this possible? I *dreamed* about her! And now she's real. What is this feeling? Is this what real love feels like? Oh my God, I don't love Claudia! How will I tell her? What will I tell our fathers?!" Like she'd done for Claudia, Valtina took all anxiety from Sebastian's mind. She also removed the thought that he should care about what the older men thought. By the time Sebastian reached home, he was happy at the thought of telling his wife he wanted a divorce.

Valtina entered the townhouse with Sebastian and watched what was possibly the most amicable breakup of all time. Claudia and Sebastian were both relieved that the other shared their feelings. They agreed that they would have no problem remaining friends and working together. They also agreed to tell their fathers to 'go to Hell.' Now that they were free, Sebastian and Claudia both wanted some alone time to fantasize about their futures. Sebastian whistled as he packed a bag and left for a hotel. Valtina planted the bar coupon on the kitchen counter and inspired a desire to go out in Claudia before following Sebastian into the car. On his way to the hotel, he called Lindsey and invited her to dinner. She answered on the first ring and arrived at the hotel only five minutes after Sebastian did.

Valtina observed the couple over dinner in the hotel restaurant. Sebastian came clean about everything… Claudia, his dream, his unexpected feelings for her. While most people would be scared off by these admissions, Lindsey wasn't like most people. She was Sebastian's soul-mate. Her heart filled with love as she listened to him. When he finished, she confessed that she'd felt the same way when she looked at him, and that she didn't care about anything else. Valtina wasn't surprised when the couple spent the night in Sebastian's room together, but didn't make love. She read Sebastian's mind and saw that he wanted to get to know Lindsey in every other way before they became physical. Unlike his father, Sebastian was an honorable man. Valtina lingered with the couple instead of checking in on Claudia. She was confident that she'd found the coupon and ended up at Albert's bar. Valtina knew that Claudia and Albert's reunion would be hot and sensual, and sometimes that was painful for Valtina to watch. She preferred Sebastian and Lindsey's peaceful, content, innocent expressions of love. Before she realized it, Valtina had spent the entire night watching the couple and reminiscing about her own soul-mate.

As dawn broke through the hotel windows, a feeling of unease filled Valtina. She'd done her job… the couple had split up, Sebastian had found Lindsey, and Claudia had realized she was still in love with Albert. But Valtina was still here… the mist had not returned to transport her home. "Damn it," Valtina thought. "Something went wrong with Claudia." She hurried back to the townhouse to evaluate the situation.

Chapter Four

Valtina returned to the townhouse and found Claudia sitting on the couch in pajamas, with empty ice cream cartons and candy packages scattered around her. The problem was clear the moment Valtina entered Claudia's mind… she was scared. Claudia was terrified of meeting Albert again. She'd spent the entire evening on the internet, scanning social media sites for information about her lost love. She discovered that he had left college a few months after they broke up, and no one had heard from him since. Valtina took away Claudia's fear and inspired her to take her trash to the kitchen. There, she noticed the bar coupon sitting on the counter. "A nice lunch and a strong drink… I think that's exactly what I need," Claudia thought. She hurried upstairs to fix herself up.

The sports bar was almost empty when Claudia entered. There were no games on, so the televisions were tuned to ESPN. Since she was dining alone, Claudia opted for a seat at the bar instead of taking up a table. She didn't want to be reminded that she had no one to sit across from her. The bartender promptly served her a martini as she scanned the menu. As she was about to order, a door by the back wall opened and a man entered.

"John, I'm still waiting for that liquor order. I need to have it faxed in by…" The bartender turned in confusion when his boss stopped abruptly, midsentence. Albert stood transfixed on the woman who'd just ordered.

"Claudia?" Albert hesitated. Claudia's eyes filled with tears.

"Hello, Albert," she replied with a teary, hopeful smile. 'What luck,' she thought to herself. 'I can't believe he's been here this whole time.'

"John, tell Marco to send two of today's specials to my office, please," Albert said softly, never moving his eyes off of Claudia. "Would you care to join me?" he asked. Claudia followed him into his office. Valtina watched the couple stumble through awkward re-introductions, which were followed by silence. Valtina inspired Claudia with a bit of bravery, and she finally spoke again.

"I've missed you, Albert," she admitted. "I don't know what happened, why you disappeared, and I don't care. I married someone else, and I missed you the whole time. I'm getting a divorce. And I'm still in love with you."

A wide smile broke across Albert's face. "I've missed you too," he said as a tear trickled down from his eye. "I don't really know what happened either," he explained. "Every time I came near you, I was overwhelmed with hopelessness. I loved you so much, and I've never stopped, but back then I had this voice in my head, telling me I'd never be good enough for you.

Eventually I listened, but Claudia, that was the worst mistake I've ever made. I've prayed every night that you'd come back to me! And now you have!" He crossed the small office and leaned down, kissing Claudia passionately. She felt as if she'd finally come home after being lost in the wilderness.

"I have an apartment upstairs," Albert breathed heavily into Claudia's ear. "I sleep here sometimes, when I have to open early. I actually lived here for a while. I built the bar before I built my house," he explained. "Would you like to see the upstairs?"

"Yes," Claudia answered huskily, impressed that Albert owned the business. She followed him to the stairs in the back corner of the office. Feeling playful, she rushed up and wrapped her arms around Albert's shoulders. He squatted, picked her up, and carried her up the stairs piggy-back like he'd always done at his dorm room. "You just wait, darlin'," he promised, "I've been dreaming about this for five years." Albert let Claudia down at the top of the stairs. The loft apartment had one room, with a queen-sized bed placed directly in front of a large entertainment center. The other side of the room held a small refrigerator, a microwave, and a small rack of clothes. Claudia assumed that the bathroom was located behind the single door in the apartment.

"You really cut to the chase, don't you?" Claudia laughed. "No couch?"

Albert laughed. "I know what this looks like, but it's not a workplace love nest… at least it hasn't been until now." He scooped Claudia up in his arms and deposited her on the bed. "You're so beautiful," he sighed. With one hand Albert caressed Claudia's face; with the other he unbuttoned her blouse. He buried his face in her breasts the moment they were free.

An electric, intoxicating tingle ran through Claudia's body. It was only then that she realized how much her body had missed Albert's touch. She scooted out of her slacks as Albert pulled her bra down and took one of her nipples in his mouth. She moaned loudly as he gently nibbled on it and then moved to the next one. Albert pulled away and she lifted his shirt over his head. He stood and quickly stepped out of his jeans before collapsing on the bed next to Claudia. They lay there for a moment, examining each other's naked bodies. The sight of Albert's fat, stiff erection made Claudia wet between the legs.

"Mmmm…" Albert moaned. "I can smell you, baby. I can smell your hot, sexy pussy. Oh how I've missed that smell… almost as much as I've missed the taste," he smiled devilishly before diving between her legs.

Claudia gasped as Albert flicked his tongue against her clit and groaned in pleasure at the taste of her juices. He lapped ferociously at her pussy and reached down to stroke his own cock. Claudia attempted to reach down and replace his hand with her own, but he pushed her away.

"Let me…" he said "All I want you to do is lie back, and let me welcome you home." Albert's breath grew heavier, and Claudia lay back and let herself fully experience the sensations of his mouth on her most sensitive spot. She let herself go, and began bucking wildly against Albert's face. As she grew to her climax, Claudia was desperate to have Albert inside of her.

"Take me, Albert," she begged. "Give me that hard, thick cock. I've missed it so much. Let me welcome it home." She raised her hips toward Albert as he climbed on top of her. He entered her slowly, just an inch at a time.

"You've missed this baby?" he prompted.

"*So* much. So much, Albert," Claudia breathed heavily. "Please, give me all of it. I need all of it." She sighed, and Albert drove himself all the way inside of her. They lay like that for a moment, connected but not moving, and then Albert started thrusting slowly. His long, full strokes provided the orgasm his tongue had begun. Claudia clinched against Albert's cock as her juices flowed over him.

"Oh baby, I think you needed that," Albert teased as he lay motionless on top of her.

"I needed you," she sighed and then kissed him hungrily. Her first release had left her wanting more, and she began grinding against Albert, squeezing his cock with her pussy muscles.

"You remember just what I like," Albert smiled. "I remember what you like too," he teased mischievously. Anticipation filled Claudia as Albert climbed off her and slid her to the edge of the bed. He stood in front of her, bending to tease her nipples again in turn. He traced his kisses up her neck and to her ear. "You know what to do baby," he whispered.

Thrilled, Claudia got on her hands and knees, her legs hanging off of the bed. Albert moved behind her, spread her legs slightly, and thrust deep inside of her. Claudia immediately felt him hit that spot, the spot deep inside her that hadn't been touched since their last encounter. This had always been her favorite position with Albert, because it allowed him to hit that spot. She braced herself with one hand and reached down to rub her clit; she used the same hand to tease Albert's balls as he moved in and out of her, just like she knew he liked it.

The sensation of Claudia's hands on his testicles almost sent Albert over the edge. He felt her pussy squeeze around his cock; Claudia's groans and cries told Albert that he had found her 'magic button.'

"Are you going to come again for me, baby?" Albert asked.

"Yes!" she cried. "Just keep doing that. Right there. Right there." She rocked back and forth on her knees, matching Albert thrust for thrust. When she finally let out the deep, whole body groan that always accompanied her orgasms, Albert let go and emptied himself inside of her. Claudia collapsed on the bed to catch her breath; Albert lay beside her.

"I'm sorry, I got carried away," Albert apologized sheepishly. "I meant to pull out. We've just found each other again… this is no time to risk a baby," he said halfheartedly, as if he needed convincing.

Claudia rolled over and looked deep into his eyes. "Why wait?" She asked simply. "I love you. I love you more deeply than I ever thought possible. I think a child made in our kind of love would be a spectacular thing. And haven't we waited long enough?"

Albert's face lit up with the purest happiness Valtina had ever seen. He opened his mouth to reply, but Valtina never heard his words. The white mist reappeared and transported her back to Middle World.

When Valtina entered Middle World, she was greeted by an irate Ladaya. "Valtina! I'm surprised at you! What in the world were you thinking? You weren't thinking, obviously, at least not about your *mission*!"

Valtina was taken aback. She had no idea what Ladaya was talking about, or why she was so upset. "Ladaya, what did I do wrong?" she asked in a panic.

"You became *distracted*! You let your mind wander. Once Sebastian and Lindsey confessed their feelings for each other, you should have *immediately* returned to Claudia. There was still plenty of time to get her to the bar that night. But instead, you sat for *hours* and daydreamed about your lost love. You delayed the completion of your mission by 14 hours! And while you were off in fantasy land, more of our numbers have fallen to evil forces. I have nine spirits unaccounted for!

The forces of evil are overpowering us, Valtina, and you're off indulging in memories of your past lives! Do you know how selfish that is?"

Shame washed over Valtina. Ladaya was right. She should have realized something was wrong with Claudia when the mist hadn't appeared. "I'm so sorry, Ladaya. I don't know what else to say." She looked down guiltily.

"You must do better next time, Valtina. You must remember the big picture, all of the others whose lives depend on your success. This is not the time for selfish, idle daydreams. Now if you'll excuse me, I must go report to MY superior. I don't know when I'll return with your next mission. While I'm gone, I'd like for you to think about how you can do better next time." And with that, Ladaya disappeared on the spot.

"I think this is going to be much, much harder than I realized," Valtina sighed out loud. She settled back under her favorite tree, but instead of studying the spirits around her, she focused on practicing her powers. She would not fail Ladaya again.

-To be continued in Book 5-

If you enjoyed this title, I would appreciate your leaving a review of the book. Good reviews encourage an author to write as well as help books to sell. Good reviews can be just a few short sentences describing what you liked about the book without having a spoiler. If you could spend 30 seconds writing a review, I would appreciate it: you can review this title right now at your favorite retailer.

Here is a preview of the **next story** you may enjoy:

Fury of Lust - The Leather Satchel Romance Series, Book 5

"**VALTINA, I'M** so sorry it took me so long to get back. My superior summoned us all to explain the new protocol. I'm afraid our forces continue to be overwhelmed by the evil armies. Two dozen spirits failed to report back after their assignments this week. Undoubtedly they've been captured by wraiths." Ladaya spoke quickly… time was not a luxury she had, given the current circumstances. She continued, "We can no longer afford to risk sending you out on your own. From now on, you will be accompanied on all of your missions by two protectors… a warrior and an emere. I've assigned Demetri as your warrior… I know you've worked well together in the past. Fatima will be your emere. She will meet you at your destination."

Valtina finally spoke. "Ladaya, what is an emere? I don't think I've ever heard you mention one before."

"I'm sorry, child. Of course you wouldn't know about emeres. The emeres are the purest form of spirits. They left the mortal world when they were infants, so their souls were never tarnished. Fatima and the other emeres have powers far more potent than even my own. And they can move freely between The Afterlife and Earth. They cannot come to Middle World, but Fatima will be able to send you home after your mission, or if you're in imminent danger. I cannot stress this enough, Valtina. You must stay vigilant and be on constant guard against danger."

Valtina was saddened by Ladaya's appearance. Gone was the carefree, wise woman who had guided her on her journey to The Afterlife. Now, Ladaya stood before her in torn robes, her hair undone and wild, and her kind eyes filled with despair. When Valtina had agreed to join the spirit army to fight against the evil forces, she'd imagined that she would receive her final reward after one or two missions. As the weeks went on, however, Valtina realized that she may never reach The Afterlife. Her destiny, it seemed, was to valiantly fight a losing battle.

"Ladaya, what can I expect to run into, besides the tricksters, succubi, and wraiths? I want to be prepared!"

"Valtina, I don't know how many kinds of monsters are now working against us. Morgonda seems to have rallied every creature that's ever been imagined. Our sources tell us that she's breeding them, combining wraith and lampades, demons and nymphs… she's designing her own unique army. I've heard she's even recruited scorned demigods to fight against us."

Valtina gasped. "Demigods? She's turning everything against us, isn't she?"

"She's doing her best to," Ladaya agreed, "but we must not be discouraged. And we must keep fighting. Are you ready for your next assignment?" Valtina responded by nodding. "I'm afraid this one may be your most challenging mission yet. You'll have Demetri and Fatima, of course, but I daresay their powers won't be much help for most of this. They're mainly along for your protection," said Ladaya.

"Ladaya, I know you've insisted on protecting me in the past, but don't Demetri and Fatima have better things to do than shadow me while I fix people's love lives? Surely they could be of more use somewhere else! I can protect myself!" Valtina insisted defiantly. It seemed to her that having two spirit babysitters was overkill. Valtina wanted to end the war as quickly as possible, so she could be reunited with her soul-mate in The Afterlife. If Demetri and Fatima worked their own assignments, they could defeat three evil situations in the time it would take them to defeat one together.

"Valtina, we are *not* arguing about this again," Ladaya answered firmly. "You may not understand your own importance, but the rest of us do. You are the culmination of every type of love that exists. *You* hold within you everything Morgonda and her armies are trying to defeat. We have other loving souls fighting for us, of course, but *you* are the most powerful. There is nothing more important than keeping you safe, and helping you to bring love back to the souls on Earth. *You* are our best chance of ridding the world from evil once and for all, Valtina!"

"Now," Ladaya continued, "your next mission. As I was saying, I'm afraid this will be your most difficult assignment yet. Rachel and Sean were supposed to meet in college and fall in love. They should have been married for six years now, but Morgonda's forces interfered. Rachel was possessed by a fury, and has been leading a dangerous, promiscuous, loveless life ever since. True love is the only power strong enough to expel a fury, so Sean has been well guarded, to ensure that the two never meet. Demons watch him day and night… study them and observe their shift schedule. You'll have to free Sean before you can help Rachel. This is a complicated case, Valtina, and we can't afford for you to become distracted like last time," Ladaya chided. Valtina blushed. During her last mission, she'd wasted nearly 14 hours daydreaming about her lives with her soul-mate. She opened her mouth to offer reassurance, but she was interrupted.

If you enjoyed this sample then look for **Fury of Lust - The Leather Satchel Romance Series, Book 5.**

Here is a preview of **another story** you may enjoy:

The Siren's Trap - The Daemon Paranormal Romance Chronicles, Book 4

PHOEBE STARED out at the ocean. In La Coruna, or A Coruna as the locals called it, the ocean was everything. Next to her was the world's oldest lighthouse. It was said to have been built by Hercules himself in ancient times. After several weeks of being in Spain and an excellent grammar book, she was finally starting to pick up on the language. Right now was not the time for studying. This moment was hers alone to stare into the great expanse of ocean before her. Across those waters, she had helped to search for a new leader, find the Qilin, and fell in love.

Already, memories were starting to float back into her mind. The spiteful witch, Juno, had taken her memories temporarily. As memories of Supay started to flow back, Phoebe realized why. Juno was not intent on leading daemons to take over the world or even gain power. They had overestimated her goals. From everything that Phoebe could figure out, Juno just wanted to cause trouble. She thrived on causing hurt to people. Although Juno had agreed to stay out of the infighting, she had managed to split Supay and Phoebe apart. Now, Phoebe was across the world with Apollo. He had rented a condo near the beach and spent each day trying to prove his love. At first, his attempts had been endearing. Now, it felt like he was smothering her. In reality, nothing may have been different. She had just started to change as her memories came back. Phoebe remembered Supay's cute quirks and his dedication to always doing what was right. She also remembered her own disapproval of Apollo and his intention to kill the Qilin. Alone at the edge of the world, there was no escape from her memories.

Picking her way down the rocks, Phoebe got as close to the ocean as possible. The few tourists that were there spoke Spanish, since La Coruna was a Spanish-tourist destination. On occasion, she ran into the random English family who had decided to take holiday there. The number of English speakers that she had met could be counted on one hand. It made for a lonely existence, but she felt less alone as her Spanish improved. The warmth of Spain and the salty sea air were a welcome change from the thin air at Cuzco.

Sitting down on a rock, Phoebe started to cry. Since finding out she was pregnant, her hormones had gone haywire. It did not help that she truly was in a bad situation. She was stuck in Spain with Apollo and could not bring herself to tell him that she was pregnant. Since she was only a few months along, it still was not noticeable. Even worse, she could not bring herself to call Supay and tell him that she was going to have their child. Unless Supay stopped by the cabin, he may not even know that she was gone. Even worse, he may have already realized she was gone. If so, he would be frantic with worry.

If you enjoyed this sample then look for **The Siren's Trap - The Daemon Paranormal Romance Chronicles, Book 4**.

Other Books by Darla Dunbar

- The Romeo Alpha BBW Paranormal Shifter Romance Series

- Romeo Alpha Blood Lines Romance Series

- The Alpha Feud BBW Paranormal Shifter Romance Series

- The Alpha Packed BBW Paranormal Shifter Romance Series

- The Daemon Paranormal Romance Chronicles

- The Mind Talker Paranormal Romance Series

Get the latest update on new releases from the author at:

https://darladunbar.com/newsletter/

About the Author - Darla Dunbar

Darla has been interested in paranormal romance since she was a teenager in high school. It was then that she discovered she could fulfill her fantasies through her writing.

Observing people and human behavior in the area of romance has always been one of her favorite pastimes. Combining that with an overactive imagination is a sure fire way of coming up with interesting themes.

Connect with Darla Dunbar

I really appreciate you reading my book! Here are my social media coordinates:

Friend me on Facebook:
https://www.facebook.com/darladunbar/

Follow me on Twitter: https://twitter.com/DarlDunbar

Check me out on Goodreads:
https://www.goodreads.com/author/show/8425857.Darl
a_Dunbar

Subscribe to my newsletter:
https://darladunbar.com/newsletter/

Visit my website: https://darladunbar.com/